Fir

MW00965543

Raffi's For
the Birds

Sylvain Meunier

Illustrated by Élisabeth Eudes-Pascal

Translated by Sarah Cummins

Formac Publishing Company Limited
Halifax

Originally published as *La paruline masquée*
Copyright © 2007 Les éditions de la courte échelle inc.
Translation Copyright © 2009 Sarah Cummins

Formac Publishing Company Limited acknowledges the support of the
Cultural Affairs Section, Nova Scotia Department of Tourism, Culture
and Heritage. We acknowledge the financial support of the
Government of Canada through the Book Publishing Industry
Development Program (BPIDP) for our publishing activities.

We acknowledge the support of the Canada Council for the Arts for
our publishing program.

Library and Archives Canada Cataloguing in Publication

Meunier, Sylvain
[Paruline masquée. English]
  Raffi's for the birds / Sylvain Meunier ; illustrations by Élisabeth
Eudes-Pascal ; translated by Sarah Cummins.
(First novels)
Translation of: La paruline masquée.
ISBN 978-0-88780-872-2 (bound)./ISBN 978-0-88780-870-8 (pbk.)

  I. Eudes-Pascal, Élisabeth II. Cummins, Sarah III. Titre.
IV. Paruline masquée. English. V. Collection: First novels

PS8576.E9P3713 2009   jC843'.54   C2009-902372-5

Formac Publishing Company Limited
5502 Atlantic Street
Halifax, NS B3H 1G4
www.formac.ca

Printed and bound in Canada

Distributed in the
United States by:
Orca Book Publishers
P.O. Box 468
Custer, WA U.S.A.
98240-0468

Table of Contents

1

An Exciting Discovery

Raffi McCaffrey had every reason to be miserable. He had a cruel enemy called sickle-cell anemia. This sickness hardly gave him a moment of peace.

But on this day, Raffi McCaffrey was as happy as a bird on the wing. In fact, he was happy *because of* a bird on the wing. He had just spotted a pair of common yellowthroats, one of the wonders of nature.

Raffi could not move around very much, so he spent most of his time sitting in front of his bedroom window. Through his binoculars, he scanned the little woodlot across from his window, looking for birds. He had seen many different kinds. One time, he had helped to save an injured purple martin.

The female yellowthroat he saw this day was very pretty, with her bright yellow throat and white breast. The male had a black mask that made him look very dashing.

Every kind of bird has its own special song. The yellowthroat is a warbler, and even though there are about thirty different kinds of warblers, each one has a song you can tell from the rest. Raffi had dozens of recordings of bird songs on his computer. When the male opened its beak to sing, Raffi imagined he could hear "*Wicheree, wicheree, wicheree!*"

Raffi never grew bored with bird-watching. There was always something new to discover, so the long time he needed to get better seemed to pass more quickly.

"Yellowthroat! That's a nice name!" exclaimed Raffi's mother.

"You don't often get to see a

yellowthroat," said Raffi. "They usually stay far away from houses where people live, and they build their nests in thick bushes."

"Yeah, fascinating," murmured his sister Serena, covering her mouth as she pretended to yawn in boredom.

Raffi's father set down his fork and finished chewing his mouthful of dinner before speaking. "Why are you making fun of Raffi, Serena? Lots of people are interested in birdwatching. It's a useful thing to do and doesn't harm anyone."

"Well, I'd like to spend my day birdwatching too, but I have to go to school!" Serena grumped in reply. "We don't all get to spend our time daydreaming and looking out

the window."

"Serena, don't be mean," their mom said. "You know that Raffi will be back in school next fall, if the blood transfusions work."

"And I still have to do my homework

every night," Raffi reminded Serena.

"I think you should apologize to Raffi," their dad told her.

"Sorry," she muttered.

"Did you do anything special today at school, Serena?" asked their mom, trying to cheer her up.

"No, not really."

2

Destruction

It was Carlito who brought Raffi his homework every day. Carlito was a year older than Raffi, but they were in the same class. He and Raffi were fast friends.

Every evening Raffi did his homework. It never took him very long.

His teacher came to the house once a week to go over his work. Ms. Troberg was

a pretty young woman, with rosy cheeks and sparkling eyes. She said that Raffi was so smart that it was a pleasure — not work — to come see him.

In the morning, Raffi's mom would help him get dressed and come downstairs for breakfast. He refused to spend all day in his pyjamas.

Afterwards, his mother went downstairs to work in her basement office. Raffi would settle in at his computer or beside the window.

This morning he was at the window, of course. He was eager for another glimpse of the yellowthroats.

Even before he raised the binoculars to his eyes, he was worried for the birds. He saw men standing at the edge of the woods. They were talking loudly. But then their voices were drowned out by a deafening racket.

Oh no! It was the motor of a chainsaw!

Raffi felt sick at heart. He trained his binoculars on the bush where the yellowthroats had built their nest.

Horror! A large man dressed in a black-and-red checked shirt and leather boots bent over and attacked the bush. He was about to cut it down to the ground.

Three other people were standing

nearby in suits, carrying papers in their hands. One of them had a big tuft of blond hair, ruffled by the wind. He seemed to be the boss. He gestured broadly in all directions, as if he intended to cut down all the trees.

Raffi could see two tiny yellow specks whirling around above the bush, as branch after branch fell to the ground. The yellowthroats were trying to chase away the intruders by dive-bombing them.

But the little creatures soon realized they were helpless against the monstrous machine that was destroying their home. They flew away before the blade could reach them too.

Raffi yelled at the top of his lungs. But his lungs were so weak that his yell was like a whisper, drowned out by the roar of the chainsaw.

Raffi's yell was just loud enough for his mother to hear. She came running up the stairs. "Raffi, what's wrong?"

"Look, Mom. They're cutting down the trees!"

His mother looked out the window. "They're only bushes, Raffi. Calm down,"

"But those are the bushes where the yellowthroats are nesting!"

"Oh. I see…." She gently stroked Raffi's hair. "That's terrible," she said sympathetically. "But don't worry too much. The birds will make another nest. Let's just hope they haven't laid their eggs yet."

"What if they don't leave any trees at all?"

"That would be very sad. But the land belongs to them. They probably want to build something there."

Raffi stared out the window with desperation in his eyes. "They can't do that! There are already enough houses around."

Raffi's mom smiled sadly. "I'm afraid there are never enough, honey."

3

Lies vs. Adventure

The day went by too slowly.

Raffi heard the sound of the chainsaw starting up several more times. Wherever it had cut down the trees and bushes, an orange stake was planted among the stumps.

Finally Raffi saw Carlito walking up the street, his pack on his back.

As he did every day, Carlito turned down the alley, went to the backyard and knocked on the kitchen door. Raffi's mom called out, "Come on in, Carlito!" She had prepared two glasses of milk and a plate of coconut cookies, which were her specialty.

Carlito was an only child and his parents always came home late from work. He would be home alone every day if he didn't come over to the McCaffreys' house. Even when Raffi went to school, Carlito always stopped by at the end of the day.

Raffi's mom carried the tray of milk and cookies up to Raffi's bedroom. Twice before, Carlito had spilled the milk when he was carrying the snack, and she figured that was enough.

★★★

Carlito gulped down his milk and devoured all of the cookies except for the one Raffi was nibbling on.

Raffi wasn't hungry. He couldn't erase from his mind the image of the yellowthroats being driven from their home. "Carlito, we have to go down to the wood."

"The wood! Your mom will never let you."

"I know. When she's down in her office, we'll tell her we're going out to play in the yard."

"It's wrong to tell a lie, Raffi."

"Carlito, I have a good reason."

Raffi told Carlito about the yellow-throats. He wanted to try to find them again. After thinking it over, Carlito decided that the adventure was worth telling a lie.

"Do you think you can walk there?" he asked Raffi.

"I'm feeling better than I have in months," Raffi assured him.

That was another lie.

★★★

"We're going out to play, Mom!"

"All right, if you feel strong enough. Just don't go near the pool," she called back.

"We won't."

Pleased that their plan was working so well, the two boys walked over to the wood.

Raffi already felt worn out, but he didn't say anything. He had spotted two straight branches lying among the debris.

He decided to use them like ski poles to help him get around.

He found the yellowthroats' cup-shaped nest, lying broken on the ground. He was relieved that there was no trace of eggs.

The two boys walked further into the wood. The bushes were taller than their heads. It was like walking through a jungle.

Carlito began to beat at the vegetation with a stick he had found, but Raffi told him to stop. They had to be as quiet as possible if they wanted to spot the yellowthroats. If they did find them, they would try to scare them away, so they would never come back to this place of danger.

"Shhh! Don't move, Carlito. Listen!"

Carlito cupped his ear with his hand.

"*Wicheree-wichereee-wicheree-wicheree!*"

"Did you hear that?" Raffi whispered. "That's the song of the yellowthroat."

"Hooray!" cried Carlito. The song stopped as soon as the cheer left his mouth.

"I told you we have to be quiet!" Raffi said crossly.

"Sorry. Now I will be quite, quite quiet."

Raffi smiled. He could always count on Carlito for a play on words.

The two boys stood silent and still for a long time. The birds seemed to be doing the same, because no singing was heard.

The woods had fallen silent. It was very strange. Raffi knew that in movies, that

always means that trouble is coming. He turned his head. He could just see the gable on the roof of his house, high above the branches. How far away it seemed!

Suddenly two yellow lines streaked over the boys' heads. It was the yellowthroats, fleeing in a flurry of feathers. Why?

Then the boys heard footsteps — heavy footsteps that made the branches crack. Through the leaves Raffi could make out a big man in a red-and-black checked shirt.

"The lumberjack!" he whispered to Carlito. "Let's get out of here!"

They ran away. At least, Carlito ran away. Raffi had hardly taken five steps before he collapsed in a heap. Carlito hurried back and helped him to his feet.

"Ow!" said Raffi, limping along beside his friend.

"Don't give up. We're nearly at the street," Carlito urged him on, pulling his hand.

But Carlito forgot to watch where he was going. He tripped on a stone and fell, pulling Raffi down with him.

They tried to get up, but it was too late. A dark shadow fell over them. They looked up. The man in the checked shirt was there. He bent over Raffi.

4

No Way!

"What exactly do you think you're doing, Raffi McCaffrey? Do you think I've got nothing better to do than go looking for you? Mom was so worried. Are you crazy or something, to just disappear like that?"

The booming voice, loud enough for everyone in the neighbourhood to hear, belonged to Serena. But suddenly

it softened.

"Oh! Hello, Mr. Neil," Serena said to the McCaffreys' neighbour, whose house was right between theirs and Carlito's.

"Mr. Neil!" said Raffi. "You're wearing a lumberjack shirt!"

"Lots of people wear checked shirts," the old man said, helping Raffi to his feet. "I didn't mean to scare you."

"He deserves to be scared!" Serena's

mood turned sour again. "What on earth were you doing here, in your condition?"

"I think the boys must have come over here for the same reason I did — to see the extent of the damage," said Mr. Neil.

"And to find the yellowthroats and try to chase them away," added Raffi.

"Are there yellowthroats here?" Mr. Neil looked surprised. "Are you sure?"

Just then, they heard "*Wicheree-wicheree-wicheree … wicheree-wicheree-wicheree!*"

"My goodness, Raffi, you're sharper than I am!" said Mr. Neil.

"It's all very nice to listen to these tweeters," said Serena crossly, "but our mother is very worried. You've seen the extent of the damage. A few weeds have been cut down. That's all. So get moving!

Time to go home!"

"I fear the situation is far more serious than that, Miss Serena," Mr. Neil corrected her.

Serena was flattered to be called "Miss" and she stopped frowning.

"There's a big sign on the other side of Maple Boulevard," Mr. Neil explained. "They're going to put up a five-storey building on this lot."

Raffi's parents were not at all happy about his adventure. "You should have told us. We would have gone over there with you."

"I didn't want to bother you," Raffi tried to excuse himself.

"Better to bother me than to cause me

such worry," his mother retorted.

"What about me? Doesn't anyone care when he bothers me?" grumbled Serena.

"I haven't forgotten what you did, Serena. But finish your dinner now. Ms. Troberg is coming over this evening, and we have to clear the table."

Raffi's teacher was always on time. She and Raffi sat together in the kitchen.

Schoolwork was soon taken care of and talk turned to the building project.

"A five-storey building!" Ms. Troberg exclaimed. "That's outrageous!"

"With an outdoor pool," Raffi's dad pointed out.

"And an underground parking garage,"

added his mom.

"It will really change the whole neighbourhood," said Ms. Troberg, who lived not far away.

Suddenly, she struck her hand on the table and straightened up, a look of determination on her face. "No way will we let this happen! We're going to do something!"

"Do what?" asked Raffi's parents.

"I was looking for a special project for the end of the year. This is perfect. The first thing we can do is write a letter to the mayor."

Serena suddenly got interested. "We could organize a demonstration."

"Whoa! Not so fast, Serena," her mother said.

"For once I have an idea, and you have to put it down," Serena sulked. "I like the little woodlot too, you know. I played there all the time when I was a kid."

Ms. Troberg smiled. "A demonstration would be great, Serena," she said. "But let's save that for the next stage. We have to be ready for a long battle, just in case."

She thought a moment, then asked Serena, "Who is your ecology teacher?"

"Uh … Mr. Bryant."

"I know him. You should to talk to him about this. I'm sure he'll want to get involved."

5

An Exchange of Letters

Dear Mr. Mayor,

My name is Raffi McCaffrey, and I live on Orchard Street. There used to be orchards in my neighbourhood, but they are gone. Now there are houses instead.

I know we need to have houses. We wouldn't want to live in caves! But maybe there are too many houses.

It's nice when streets are named after trees and orchards. But if we keep cutting down the trees, there will be nothing left but hydro poles.

I am sick and can't go to school, so I spend a lot of time looking at the woodlot between Orchard Street and Maple Boulevard.

Did you know that many species of birds live there? I have seen yellowthroats there. Their nest was destroyed by the lumberjack.

The yellowthroats won't come back, and that makes me sad. Other people will also be sad if the woods are replaced by an apartment building. Bricks and cars don't make people happy, but birds do.

I looked on the Internet and I saw that there are many apartments for sale in our town. There are even more available in the city. But many bird species are threatened with extinction.

Mr. Mayor, to destroy our woodlot would be an ECOLOGICAL DISASTER. *Instead, we should help our environment by cleaning it up.*

Thank you for your attention.

Raffi McCaffrey

★★★

Dear Raffi,

Thank you for your letter, which I read very carefully. Unfortunately, it is beyond my power to change the course of things. The land you wrote about does not belong to the town. The owners of these lots have obtained the permits for construction they need to build there.

These are responsible people. Their building will help the economy and the town.

I know this will not benefit the birds, but they will find another place to live. New trees will be planted around the building.

One day when you're older and understand the economy better, you will be happy to see birds in these trees.

I hope you keep up with your birdwatching, a very enjoyable recreational activity.

Reginald Regimbald
Mayor of Pine Ridge

"That is pathetic!" exclaimed Ms. Troberg,

reading the mayor's letter. "He just doesn't get it. Every pupil in my class wrote him a letter like Raffi's. Everyone got exactly the same letter back, down to the last comma. The mayor doesn't seem to care."

Ms. Troberg was sitting at the kitchen table with Raffi and his family, except for his mother. She was downstairs in her office, looking something up on the computer.

"Got it!" Raffi's mom cried, as she came into the room. "The work is going to start next Monday. There will be a ground-breaking ceremony to launch the project."

"Monday! That gives us just enough time to get organized," said Ms. Troberg. "Serena, have you talked to Mr. Bryant?"

"Yes, I have," said Serena, "He's taking a

class outing to the woods. We're going to record as many species of birds and trees as we can."

"Great. Has a date been set?"

"I don't think so."

"I'll call him and see if it can be arranged for next Monday. And I myself am going to put together a nice surprise for Mr. Mayor."

6

The Yellowthroats' Counterattack

On Monday Raffi was awakened by the sound of heavy machinery driving up to the edge of the woodlot. There was a dump truck, a hydraulic shovel and a bulldozer. The name *John Hammer Enterprises* was written on each of them.

The big yellow machines were

impressive. Raffi had always dreamed of driving one. Only he had imagined himself on a building site, not in a woodlot attacking innocent plants and animals.

The operators of this scary equipment were standing around chatting while they waited for the ceremony to begin.

"They're here," said Raffi's parents, coming into his room. "Let's get ready."

It was a warm sunny day. It felt like summer vacation already.

Other workers arrived and set up a red ribbon. One of them was carrying a sparkly golden shovel. A police car was parked off to the side.

There was the man with blond hair Raffi had seen before. Several other men and women in fancy clothes were with him.

There were a few reporters too. Cameras in hand, they hurried over to the mayor's car. The mayor got out and began to shake hands all around.

Once these formalities were out of the way, everyone went and stood in front of the ribbon. The mayor got ready to deliver his speech.

Few people noticed Raffi and his parents arriving. Raffi was so nervous that he had to walk with crutches. Mr. and Mrs. Neil joined them. No one paid them much attention.

People began to take notice when a merry band of about thirty teenagers arrived on the scene. They were led by a young man with curly hair and a thick

beard. It was Mr. Bryant and his class. Serena walked next to her teacher, as proud as an Amazon warrior.

Each student had a notebook and a pen. All the cameras immediately turned towards them. This did not please Mr. Mayor.

A police officer got out of her car and shouted at Mr. Bryant to clear away from the ceremony.

"This isn't a demonstration," he protested. "My class is here to carry out an ecological survey. We are going to identify all the trees growing in this natural habitat."

The police officer was not quite sure what she should do, especially as the reporters were crowding around with their microphones. There was even a television camera filming everything.

The man with the blond tuft of hair stepped forward. "This is private property, sir! It belongs to me. I intend to get the work started. Please return to your classroom."

But he spoke too late. Led by Serena, the students were already fanning out in the woods. They began picking up fallen leaves and sketching the trees.

The mayor tried to calm down the man with the blond hair. "They won't be here all day, Mr. Hammer. Let's just start the ceremony."

The mayor had no idea there was another surprise in store for him.

A joyful song suddenly rang out:

"*W i c h e r e e - w i c h e r e e - w i c h e r e e !*
W i c h e r e e - w i c h e r e e - w i c h e r e e !"

A flock of giant yellowthroats came around the corner and joined the gathering.

"What's this?" demanded the mayor.

"It's the counterattack of the yellowthroats!" Ms. Troberg said, loud and clear.

Each of her pupils was wearing a black-

and-yellow mask, just like the one that marked the male yellowthroat's face. Raffi picked out Carlito, who waved at him. The whole group kept singing at the top of their voices.

"*Wicheree-wicheree-wicheree! Wicheree-wicheree-wicheree!*"

"I suppose your class is here for a science project too!" said Mr. Hammer, barely keeping his temper.

"No, we're not," Ms. Troberg replied sweetly. "We've come to play hide-and-seek. Let's go, kids!"

At the signal, all the giant yellow-throats ran to hide in the woods, flapping their wings and singing, "*Wicheree-wicheree-wicheree! Wicheree-wicheree-wicheree!*"

Mr. Hammer was beside himself.

"Mr. Mayor! Call police officers and have them take these vermin away. I am the owner of this land, and I intend to start work on it."

The mayor looked like he had swallowed a bug. "Vermin! Really, Mr. Hammer, you can't…. They are children, after all."

The police officer took off her helmet and scratched her head under her blonde curls. The reporters were filming and recording everyone's reactions. The workers waited, leaning against their machine. One city official nervously rubbed the golden shovel over and over.

Then Raffi stepped forward, with his parents and his neighbours.

"Gentlemen, my son has something he would like to say," said Mr. McCaffrey clearly.

The reporters immediately gathered around the strange boy, whose head seemed too big for his puny body.

Raffi took a sheet of paper from his pocket. He had prepared well. He spoke with all the force he could muster from his weakened lungs.

"Birds do not belong to anyone. Birds bring us happiness and ask for nothing in return. They like to live among humans, but humans must leave them enough room to live. Nature belongs to everyone, and we, the citizens of Pine Ridge, want this woodlot to be protected."

When Raffi had finished, Mr. Neil

presented the mayor with a petition — a resolution to protect the woodlot, signed by dozens of people.

★★★

That evening, the McCaffrey family

gathered in the living room to watch the news.

"Now, let's go to Pine Ridge," said the announcer, "and our reporter Lily Laflamme. Lily, a lot seems to be happening in this little town."

"That's right, Peter. This morning, several citizens and dozens of pupils from nearby schools mobilized to stop the destruction of a small woodlot…."

The flock of giant yellowthroats appeared on the screen, singing their joyful song: "*Wicheree-wicheree-wicheree! Wicheree-wicheree-wicheree!*"

Then there was Raffi, describing the common yellowthroat to a fascinated reporter.

Next up was the mayor, looking embarrassed. He said that his government was well aware of the importance of protecting green spaces. Over the song of the yellowthroats, he promised that they would take another look at the building project.

"Builder John Hammer declined to answer our questions and left the site, to the applause of the schoolchildren," Lily Laflamme said in conclusion.

"Regardless of the outcome, you have shown us an extraordinary and very impressive young man!" said the anchor, before moving on to the next story.

"Wouldn't you know it?" grumbled Serena. "Little brother steals the show again."

"The important thing is that we won," said Mr. McCaffrey. "And to celebrate that, I propose a trip to the ice-cream store. My treat!"

"Sounds great!" For once, Serena looked happy.

It was still light outside when they got into the car.

"Wait a sec!" said Raffi suddenly. "Listen!"

They all fell silent.

"*Wicheree-wicheree-wicheree! Wicheree-wicheree-wicheree!*"

Raffi put his hand above his eyes and looked around.

"There!" he cried. He pointed to the other side of the street. On the end of a branch, two yellow specks shone in the rays of the setting sun.

"They've come back!"

More novels in the *First Novels* series!

Daredevil Morgan

Ted Staunton

Illustrated by Bill Slavin

Morgan's best friend Charlie urges him to try the GraviTwirl ride at the Fall Fair. But Morgan is focused on the huge contender he has grown for the Perfect Pumpkin contest. That is, until Aldeen Hummel, the Godzilla of Grade Three, drops it!

Morgan challenges Aldeen to bumper car wars. Aldeen dares him to go on the Asteroid Belt ride. Will Morgan be brave enough to try? And will Morgan win the

Best Pumpkin Pie contest with the remains of his squished squash?

Mia, Matt and the Pigs that Sing

Annie Langlois

Illustrated by Jimmy Beaulieu

Translated by Sarah Cummins

Each summer, twins Mia and Matt spend their vacation at the cottage, along a lake with their uncle Orlando. The cottage — really a small farm — is where Uncle Orlando trains animals for movies and TV shows. Last summer, he trained Alfred the Turkey for a movie. This year, Mia and Matt are in for a challenge — to help teach a chorus of pigs to sing! Will Mia and Matt be able to teach Do, Re, Me, Fa, Sol, La and Ti to perform, or will the pigs live up to their stubborn nature?

Captain Lilly and the New Girl
Brenda Bellingham
Illustrated by Clarke MacDonald

Lilly is excited about playing with the community league girls' soccer team. When the new girl, Sara, joins the team, there is controversy over her headscarf caused by their competing team's coach. The Wolves band together and insist that if Sara can't play with her hijab, they will not play at all.